# Slavery's Shadows

## America literature: 19th century, Volume 1

Nora Hayes

Published by Nora Hayes, 2024.

SLAVERY'S SHADOWS

**First edition. May 5, 2024.**

Copyright © 2024 Nora Hayes.

ISBN: 979-8224528516

Written by Nora Hayes.

# Table of Contents

To those whose voices were silenced by oppression,

To those whose stories were buried by history,

To those whose resilience shines through the shadows
of adversity,

This book is dedicated.

May your courage and resilience inspire us to confront
injustice,

May your stories be heard and honored,

May your legacy of resistance illuminate the path
toward a more just and equitable future.

With gratitude and reverence,

Nora Hayes

# Chapter 1: Introduction

## Setting the stage: Overview of slavery in 19th-century America

Slavery in America during the 19th century was a deeply entrenched institution that shaped every aspect of society, economy, and culture. Originating from the colonial era and persisting until the Civil War, slavery formed the foundation of the Southern agricultural economy, providing cheap labor for plantations that produced lucrative cash crops such as cotton, tobacco, and sugar cane. The system of slavery also extended into the Northern states, albeit to a lesser extent, where enslaved individuals were utilized in various industries and domestic work.

By the 19th century, the United States had become deeply divided over the issue of slavery. The abolitionist movement gained momentum, fueled by moral outrage over the brutal treatment of enslaved people and the violation of their basic human rights. On the other hand, defenders of slavery argued for its economic necessity and upheld racist ideologies to justify the subjugation of African Americans.

The legal framework supporting slavery was codified in the United States Constitution, with the infamous Three-Fifths Compromise counting enslaved individuals as three-fifths of a person for the purposes of representation in Congress. The Fugitive Slave Act of 1850 further entrenched the institution by compelling citizens to assist in the capture and return of escaped slaves, even in free states.

Despite the harsh realities of slavery, enslaved individuals resisted their oppression through various means. From acts of rebellion and escape to covert forms of resistance such as sabotage and feigning illness, enslaved people demonstrated remarkable resilience in the face of adversity.

# Brief discussion on the significance of literature in documenting resistance and resilience

Literature played a crucial role in documenting the experiences of enslaved individuals and capturing the spirit of resistance and resilience that characterized their lives. While many aspects of enslaved life were intentionally obscured or misrepresented by pro-slavery forces, literature provided a platform for enslaved individuals to tell their own stories, assert their humanity, and challenge the dominant narratives of the time.

Slave narratives, autobiographical accounts written by formerly enslaved individuals, offered firsthand testimonies of the horrors of slavery and the quest for freedom. These narratives, often published with the assistance of abolitionist editors, provided valuable insights into the daily lives, struggles, and triumphs of enslaved people.

In addition to slave narratives, literature of the 19th century encompassed a wide range of genres and forms that addressed the issue of slavery and its impact on American society. Fictional works such as Harriet Beecher Stowe's "Uncle Tom's Cabin" and Frederick Douglass's "The Heroic Slave" used narrative storytelling to expose the brutality of slavery and advocate for its abolition.

Poetry also emerged as a powerful medium for expressing resistance and resilience in the face of oppression. Poets such as Phillis Wheatley, Frances Ellen Watkins Harper, and Paul Laurence Dunbar used their verse to challenge the dehumanization of enslaved people and celebrate their strength and dignity.

Religious texts and spirituals provided solace and inspiration to enslaved individuals, serving as a source of hope and liberation in the midst of suffering. These forms of literature reflected the deep spiritual resilience of enslaved communities and their enduring faith in the promise of freedom.

Overall, literature of the 19th century serves as a testament to the indomitable spirit of enslaved individuals and their relentless pursuit of freedom and justice. By documenting their stories of resistance and resilience, literature not only bears witness to the atrocities of slavery but also inspires future generations to continue the fight for equality and human rights.

# Chapter 2: Roots of Resistance

## Exploration of early literary works by enslaved individuals

The roots of resistance against slavery in America run deep, and one of the most powerful forms of resistance emerged through the literary expressions of enslaved individuals themselves. Despite the oppressive conditions they faced, many enslaved people found ways to assert their humanity and agency through various forms of creative expression. These early literary works offer invaluable insights into the lived experiences of enslaved individuals and the complex strategies they employed to resist their oppression.

One of the earliest forms of literary expression among enslaved individuals was the spiritual. Rooted in African religious traditions and adapted to the harsh realities of slavery, spirituals served as both a form of worship and a means of communication and resistance. These songs often contained coded messages and double entendres that conveyed messages of hope, freedom, and defiance to those who understood their hidden meanings. Spirituals such as "Go Down Moses," "Swing Low, Sweet Chariot," and "Wade in the Water" became anthems of resistance, inspiring enslaved people to persevere in the face of adversity.

In addition to spirituals, enslaved individuals also utilized folk songs and oral traditions as forms of resistance. Through storytelling, music, and performance, enslaved communities preserved their cultural heritage, transmitted valuable knowledge and wisdom, and subverted the dominant narratives of slavery. Folk tales, legends, and jokes served as both entertainment and critique, offering a space for enslaved individuals to express their creativity and resilience in the face of oppression.

# Analysis of spirituals, folk songs, and oral traditions as forms of resistance

Spirituals, folk songs, and oral traditions played a central role in the resistance efforts of enslaved individuals, serving as powerful tools for preserving cultural identity, fostering community solidarity, and expressing dissent against the institution of slavery. Through a careful analysis of these forms of expression, we can gain a deeper understanding of the ways in which enslaved people resisted their oppression and asserted their humanity.

Spirituals, with their rich blend of African rhythms, Christian imagery, and coded language, served multiple functions within the enslaved community. On one level, they provided a means of spiritual expression and comfort in the midst of suffering, offering solace and hope to those enduring the hardships of slavery. At the same time, spirituals also served as a form of resistance, conveying messages of liberation and defiance that challenged the authority of slaveholders and asserted the humanity of enslaved individuals.

For example, songs like "Follow the Drinking Gourd" provided practical guidance for enslaved individuals seeking to escape to freedom, using celestial navigation as a metaphor for the Underground Railroad. Similarly, songs like "Steal Away" and "Swing Low, Sweet Chariot" expressed longing for freedom and deliverance, while also evoking images of divine intervention and justice.

Folk songs and oral traditions likewise served as vehicles for resistance and resilience within enslaved communities. Through call-and-response chants, work songs, and field hollers, enslaved individuals found ways to maintain their cultural traditions, build solidarity, and express their grievances in a manner that circumvented the watchful eyes of slaveholders. These songs often contained veiled critiques of the slave system, celebrating the strength and ingenuity of enslaved people while lamenting the injustices they endured.

In addition to music, storytelling played a crucial role in preserving cultural memory and fostering resistance among enslaved communities. Through folk tales, legends, and myths, enslaved individuals passed down valuable knowledge, moral lessons, and subversive messages that challenged the dehumanizing narratives of slavery. By reclaiming their own stories and asserting their agency as storytellers, enslaved people resisted the erasure of their humanity and asserted their right to self-determination.

In conclusion, spirituals, folk songs, and oral traditions were powerful forms of resistance and resilience within enslaved communities, providing a means of cultural expression, spiritual sustenance, and collective solidarity in the face of oppression. Through their music, stories, and traditions, enslaved individuals forged bonds of resistance that sustained them in their struggle for freedom and dignity.

# Chapter 3: Slave Narratives: Voices of the Oppressed

Slave narratives stand as powerful testimonies to the lived experiences of enslaved individuals in 19th-century America. These autobiographical accounts offer firsthand insights into the horrors of slavery, the resilience of the human spirit, and the quest for freedom and dignity in the face of oppression. Through a close examination of prominent slave narratives such as "Narrative of the Life of Frederick Douglass" and "Incidents in the Life of a Slave Girl," we can gain a deeper understanding of the brutality of slavery and the role of narrative in inspiring abolitionist movements.

## 1. Introduction to Slave Narratives

- **Overview of the genre:** Slave narratives are autobiographical accounts written by formerly enslaved individuals, often with the assistance of abolitionist editors. They provide detailed descriptions of the author's experiences as a slave, including their treatment, living conditions, and attempts to escape to freedom.

- **Importance of slave narratives**: Slave narratives played a crucial role in exposing the atrocities of slavery to a wider audience and galvanizing support for the abolitionist cause. By bearing witness to their own suffering and resilience, enslaved individuals challenged the dehumanizing narratives perpetuated by slaveholders and inspired others to join the fight against slavery.

# 2. "Narrative of the Life of Frederick Douglass, an American Slave"

- **Biography of Frederick Douglass:** Born into slavery in Maryland, Frederick Douglass escaped to freedom and became one of the leading abolitionists of his time. His narrative is one of the most widely read and influential accounts of slavery in American history.

- **Analysis of key themes:** Douglass's narrative exposes the hypocrisy of American democracy and the brutal realities of slavery. He vividly describes the physical and psychological abuses inflicted upon enslaved individuals, as well as the ways in which slavery dehumanizes both the enslaved and the enslavers.

- **Narrative strategies:** Douglass's narrative employs a straightforward and unflinching style, characterized by vivid imagery and powerful rhetoric. His use of personal anecdotes and rhetorical devices such as irony and repetition effectively conveys the horrors of slavery and calls into question the morality of the institution.

# 3. "Incidents in the Life of a Slave Girl" by Harriet Jacobs

- **Biography of Harriet Jacobs:** Harriet Jacobs, writing under the pseudonym Linda Brent, was born into slavery in North Carolina. Her narrative, published in 1861, provides a rare female perspective on the institution of slavery and the struggles of enslaved women.

- **Analysis of key themes:** Jacobs's narrative focuses on the experiences of enslaved women, including the sexual exploitation and abuse they endured at the hands of their masters. She also highlights the complex moral dilemmas faced by enslaved individuals, particularly women, who were forced to navigate the oppressive confines of slavery while striving to protect themselves and their loved ones.

- **Narrative strategies:** Jacobs's narrative combines elements of autobiography, fiction, and political manifesto. Through her use of pseudonyms and composite characters, she protects the identities of herself and her family while also presenting a compelling and emotionally resonant account of her experiences. Her narrative is characterized by its intimate tone, moral clarity, and unwavering commitment to justice.

# 4. Role of Narrative in Abolitionist Movements

- **Influence of slave narratives:** Slave narratives played a central role in shaping public opinion and mobilizing support for the abolitionist cause. By offering firsthand testimonies of the horrors of slavery, these narratives challenged the myths and stereotypes that perpetuated the institution and inspired readers to take action against it.

- **Impact on abolitionist rhetoric:** The publication of slave narratives provided abolitionist leaders with powerful rhetorical tools to advocate for the end of slavery. Figures such as Frederick Douglass and Harriet Jacobs became outspoken critics of slavery, using their own experiences as evidence of its inherent cruelty and injustice.

- **Legacy of slave narratives**: Although slavery was officially abolished with the ratification of the 13th Amendment in 1865, the legacy of slave narratives continues to resonate today. These accounts serve as a reminder of the enduring struggle for freedom and equality and inspire contemporary movements for social justice and human rights.

In conclusion, slave narratives such as "Narrative of the Life of Frederick Douglass" and "Incidents in the Life of a Slave Girl" provide invaluable insights into the experiences of enslaved individuals and the brutal realities of slavery in 19th-century America. Through their vivid descriptions, personal anecdotes, and unwavering commitment to justice, these narratives not only exposed the atrocities of slavery but also inspired generations of abolitionists to fight for freedom and equality for all.

# Chapter 4: Abolitionist Literature

Abolitionist literature played a pivotal role in the fight against slavery in 19th-century America. Written by activists, intellectuals, and formerly enslaved individuals, these works advocated for the immediate and complete abolition of slavery, exposed the brutality of the institution, and called upon readers to join the cause of freedom and justice. In this chapter, we will survey the landscape of abolitionist literature and analyze works by key authors such as Harriet Beecher Stowe, William Lloyd Garrison, and Harriet Tubman.

## 1. Introduction to Abolitionist Literature

- **Overview of the abolitionist movement**: The abolitionist movement emerged in the early 19th century as a response to the injustices of slavery. Abolitionists sought to eradicate slavery entirely, viewing it as a moral evil that violated the principles of freedom and equality enshrined in the Declaration of Independence.

  - **Role of literature in the abolitionist cause:** Abolitionist literature served as a powerful tool for raising awareness, mobilizing support, and challenging the pro-slavery narratives that justified the institution. Through novels, newspapers, pamphlets, and speeches, abolitionist writers sought to sway public opinion and galvanize action against slavery.

# 2. "Uncle Tom's Cabin" by Harriet Beecher Stowe

- **Biography of Harriet Beecher Stowe:** Harriet Beecher Stowe was a white abolitionist and author who wrote "Uncle Tom's Cabin" in 1852. The novel became one of the most influential works of abolitionist literature and contributed significantly to the escalation of tensions leading to the Civil War.

   - **Analysis of key themes:** "Uncle Tom's Cabin" tells the story of Tom, an enslaved man, and his struggles against the cruelty of his master, Simon Legree. Through vivid characters and dramatic plotlines, Stowe exposes the inhumanity of slavery, challenges racial stereotypes, and calls upon readers to confront the moral implications of their complicity in the slave system.

   - **Impact of the novel:** "Uncle Tom's Cabin" was a runaway bestseller, selling over 300,000 copies in its first year of publication and inspiring countless readers to join the abolitionist cause. The novel sparked heated debates over the morality of slavery and helped to shift public opinion in favor of abolition.

# 3. The Liberator and William Lloyd Garrison

- **Biography of William Lloyd Garrison:** William Lloyd Garrison was a white abolitionist and journalist who founded the anti-slavery newspaper "The Liberator" in 1831. Through his writings and speeches, Garrison became one of the most prominent and uncompromising voices of the abolitionist movement.

- **Analysis of key themes**: "The Liberator" served as a platform for Garrison to denounce slavery as a moral abomination and demand its immediate abolition. Garrison's uncompromising rhetoric and radical stance on nonviolence and moral suasion earned him both admirers and detractors within the abolitionist movement.

- **Impact of the newspaper**: "The Liberator" played a crucial role in shaping the agenda of the abolitionist movement and rallying support for its cause. Garrison used the newspaper to advocate for a wide range of social justice issues, including women's rights, temperance, and pacifism, making it a hub for progressive activism in the antebellum United States.

# 4. Harriet Tubman and the Underground Railroad

- **Biography of Harriet Tubman:** Harriet Tubman was an African American abolitionist and conductor on the Underground Railroad, a network of secret routes and safe houses that helped enslaved individuals escape to freedom. Tubman's bravery and ingenuity made her a legendary figure in the fight against slavery.

- **Analysis of Tubman's contributions**: Although Tubman was not a writer in the traditional sense, her actions spoke volumes about the resilience and determination of enslaved individuals to resist their oppression. Through her daring rescues and fearless leadership, Tubman became a symbol of hope and inspiration for countless enslaved people seeking freedom.

- **Legacy of Tubman's activism:** Tubman's legacy as a freedom fighter and humanitarian endures to this day, inspiring generations of activists to continue the struggle for equality and justice. Her life and legacy serve as a reminder of the power of individual agency and collective action in the fight against injustice.

# 5. Conclusion

- **Recap of key themes and contributions:** Abolitionist literature played a crucial role in exposing the horrors of slavery, mobilizing support for the abolitionist cause, and ultimately bringing about the end of slavery in the United States. Through novels, newspapers, speeches, and personal narratives, abolitionist writers challenged the moral legitimacy of slavery and called upon readers to join the fight for freedom and equality.

- **Reflection on the enduring relevance of abolitionist literature**: While slavery may have been abolished formally with the ratification of the 13th Amendment in 1865, the legacy of abolitionist literature continues to resonate in contemporary struggles for social justice and human rights. The works of writers like Harriet Beecher Stowe, William Lloyd Garrison, and Harriet Tubman serve as timeless reminders of the power of literature to effect change and inspire movements for liberation.

In conclusion, abolitionist literature played a crucial role in the fight against slavery, exposing its horrors, mobilizing support for its abolition, and inspiring generations of activists to continue the struggle for freedom and equality. Through novels, newspapers, speeches, and personal narratives, abolitionist writers challenged the moral legitimacy of slavery and called upon readers to join the fight for justice and human rights.

# Chapter 5: The Power of Fiction

Fictional literature has long served as a powerful vehicle for exploring complex social issues, challenging prevailing norms, and inspiring change. In the context of slavery in 19th and 20th-century America, novels addressing themes of slavery and resistance played a crucial role in shaping public perception, sparking debates, and contributing to social change. In this chapter, we will explore the impact of fictional works such as "Uncle Tom's Cabin" by Harriet Beecher Stowe and "Beloved" by Toni Morrison on public perception and social change.

## 1. Introduction to Fictional Literature on Slavery

**- Overview of the role of fiction in addressing social issues:** Fictional literature has the unique ability to engage readers emotionally and intellectually, inviting them to empathize with characters and situations that may be unfamiliar or uncomfortable. In the context of slavery, fictional works provide a lens through which readers can explore the complexities of power, oppression, and resistance.

- **Importance of representation:** Fictional literature on slavery offers a platform for marginalized voices to tell their own stories, reclaim their agency, and challenge dominant narratives. By centering the experiences of enslaved individuals, these novels humanize the victims of slavery and underscore the inherent dignity and humanity of all people.

# 2. "Uncle Tom's Cabin" by Harriet Beecher Stowe

- **Biography of Harriet Beecher Stowe:** Harriet Beecher Stowe was a white abolitionist and author who wrote "Uncle Tom's Cabin" in 1852. The novel, serialized in an abolitionist newspaper before being published in book form, became one of the most influential works of fiction in American history.

- **Analysis of key themes:** "Uncle Tom's Cabin" tells the story of Tom, an enslaved man, and his struggles against the cruelty of his master, Simon Legree. Through vivid characters and dramatic plotlines, Stowe exposes the inhumanity of slavery, challenges racial stereotypes, and calls upon readers to confront the moral implications of their complicity in the slave system.

- **Impact of the novel:** "Uncle Tom's Cabin" was a cultural sensation, selling over 300,000 copies in its first year of publication and inspiring countless readers to join the abolitionist cause. The novel sparked heated debates over the morality of slavery and helped to shift public opinion in favor of abolition. It also played a significant role in escalating tensions leading to the Civil War, earning Stowe praise from abolitionist leaders and condemnation from pro-slavery forces.

# 3. "Beloved" by Toni Morrison

- **Biography of Toni Morrison:** Toni Morrison was an African American author and Nobel laureate known for her powerful explorations of race, identity, and memory in American society. "Beloved," published in 1987, is widely regarded as one of her masterpieces and a seminal work of American literature.

- **Analysis of key themes:** "Beloved" tells the story of Sethe, an escaped enslaved woman, and her struggles to rebuild her life in the aftermath of slavery. The novel delves into themes of trauma, memory, and the legacy of slavery, as Sethe confronts the ghosts of her past and grapples with the meaning of freedom and redemption.

- **Impact of the novel**: "Beloved" received widespread critical acclaim and won the Pulitzer Prize for Fiction in 1988. The novel's visceral depiction of the horrors of slavery and its exploration of the psychological and emotional toll of oppression resonated deeply with readers, sparking discussions about the legacies of slavery and the ongoing struggles for racial justice in America. "Beloved" remains a staple of college and university curricula, continuing to inspire readers to confront uncomfortable truths about America's past and present.

# 4. Discussion on the Impact of Fictional Literature on Public Perception and Social Change

- **Influence on public perception:** Fictional literature on slavery has played a crucial role in shaping public perception and understanding of the institution. By offering nuanced portrayals of enslaved individuals and their experiences, these novels challenge stereotypes and misconceptions, fostering empathy and compassion among readers.

- **Contribution to social change:** Fictional literature has the power to ignite conversations, mobilize communities, and inspire collective action. Novels such as "Uncle Tom's Cabin" and "Beloved" have sparked debates about the legacies of slavery, the persistence of racial inequality, and the ongoing struggles for justice and liberation. By shedding light on the injustices of the past, these novels invite readers to reflect on their own roles in shaping a more equitable and just society.

# 5. Conclusion

- **Recap of key themes and contributions:** Fictional literature on slavery has played a crucial role in shaping public perception, sparking debates, and contributing to social change. Novels such as "Uncle Tom's Cabin" and "Beloved" offer nuanced portrayals of the complexities of slavery, challenging stereotypes and inspiring readers to confront uncomfortable truths about America's past and present.

- **Reflection on the enduring relevance of fiction:** While slavery may have been formally abolished with the ratification of the 13th Amendment, the legacies of slavery continue to shape American society in profound ways. Fictional literature serves as a reminder of the enduring struggles for freedom and justice and an invitation to imagine new possibilities for a more equitable and inclusive future.

# Chapter 6: Poetry of Protest

Poetry has long served as a potent medium for expressing dissent, resistance, and resilience in the face of oppression. In the context of slavery in 19th and early 20th-century America, poetry emerged as a powerful tool for enslaved individuals and abolitionist writers to confront the horrors of slavery, assert their humanity, and inspire social change. In this chapter, we will examine the poetry of protest, focusing on the works of poets such as Phillis Wheatley, Frances Ellen Watkins Harper, and Paul Laurence Dunbar.

## 1. Introduction to Poetry of Protest

- **Overview of the role of poetry in protest**: Poetry has the unique ability to distill complex emotions and experiences into concise and evocative language, making it an effective medium for expressing resistance and resilience. In the context of slavery, poetry provided a means for enslaved individuals and abolitionist writers to voice their grievances, assert their humanity, and challenge the dehumanizing narratives of slavery.

- **Importance of oral tradition**: Many enslaved individuals were unable to read or write, making oral forms of expression such as poetry and song particularly important in preserving cultural memory and fostering community solidarity. Through call-and-response chants, work songs, and spirituals, enslaved communities maintained their cultural traditions and transmitted messages of resistance and resilience.

# 2. Phillis Wheatley: A Trailblazer in Poetry

- **Biography of Phillis Wheatley**: Phillis Wheatley was an enslaved African woman who became the first published African American poet in 1773. Despite the limitations imposed by her enslaved status, Wheatley's talent and intellect attracted the attention of prominent figures in colonial America, leading to the publication of her poetry collection, "Poems on Various Subjects, Religious and Moral."

- **Analysis of key themes**: Wheatley's poetry explores themes of faith, freedom, and the human condition, drawing on classical forms and Christian imagery to convey her experiences as an enslaved individual. Her poems often serve as subtle critiques of the institution of slavery, challenging the hypocrisy of slaveholders and calling for justice and equality.

- **Impact of her work**: Wheatley's poetry challenged prevailing stereotypes of African Americans as intellectually inferior and demonstrated the capacity of enslaved individuals for artistic expression and intellectual achievement. Her success as a poet paved the way for future generations of African American writers and poets, inspiring them to assert their own voices and perspectives.

# 3. Frances Ellen Watkins Harper: A Voice for Justice

- **Biography of Frances Ellen Watkins Harper**: Frances Ellen Watkins Harper was an African American poet, abolitionist, and women's rights activist who rose to prominence in the mid-19th century. Born free in Maryland, Harper used her poetry to advocate for the abolition of slavery, the rights of women, and the dignity and equality of all people.

- **Analysis of key themes**: Harper's poetry addresses a wide range of social justice issues, including slavery, racism, sexism, and economic inequality. Her poems are characterized by their passionate advocacy for the oppressed and their call to action for social change. Harper's use of vivid imagery, rhythmic language, and emotional intensity captivates readers and inspires them to join the fight for justice.

- **Impact of her work**: Harper's poetry was widely circulated in abolitionist newspapers and anthologies, reaching audiences across the country and galvanizing support for the abolitionist cause. Her powerful words resonated with readers of all backgrounds, challenging them to confront the injustices of their society and work towards a more equitable and just future.

# 4. Paul Laurence Dunbar: A Poet of the People

- **Biography of Paul Laurence Dunbar**: Paul Laurence Dunbar was an African American poet, novelist, and playwright who gained national acclaim in the late 19th and early 20th centuries. Born to formerly enslaved parents in Ohio, Dunbar drew on his experiences growing up in the post-Civil War South to write poetry that celebrated the beauty and resilience of African American culture.

- **Analysis of key themes**: Dunbar's poetry explores themes of love, loss, identity, and racial pride, capturing the richness and complexity of African American life. His use of dialect and vernacular language adds authenticity and depth to his poems, allowing readers to connect with the experiences of African Americans in a deeply personal way.

- **Impact of his work**: Dunbar's poetry resonated with readers of all backgrounds, earning him widespread acclaim as the "poet laureate of the Negro race." His poems were published in newspapers and anthologies, reaching audiences across the country and beyond. Dunbar's celebration of African American culture and resilience inspired generations of writers and poets to embrace their own cultural heritage and assert their voices in the literary world.

# 5. Conclusion

- **Recap of key themes and contributions:** Poetry of protest played a crucial role in expressing resistance and resilience in the face of slavery and oppression. Poets such as Phillis Wheatley, Frances Ellen Watkins Harper, and Paul Laurence Dunbar used their words to challenge injustice, inspire change, and celebrate the beauty and resilience of the human spirit. Through their poetry, they asserted their humanity, reclaimed their voices, and paved the way for future generations to continue the fight for justice and equality.

- **Reflection on the enduring relevance of poetry:** Poetry continues to serve as a powerful medium for expressing protest, resistance, and resilience in the face of injustice. The works of poets such as Wheatley, Harper, and Dunbar remind us of the power of language to inspire change and challenge the status quo, inviting readers to join the ongoing struggle for freedom, justice, and equality.

# Chapter 7: Emancipation and Reconstruction

The period of Emancipation and Reconstruction following the Civil War marked a significant turning point in American history, particularly for formerly enslaved individuals. Literature produced during and after this tumultuous era offers invaluable insights into the struggles, triumphs, and complex legacies of emancipation and Reconstruction. In this chapter, we will explore the literature of this period, focusing on narratives that document the experiences of formerly enslaved individuals.

## 1. Introduction to Emancipation and Reconstruction

- **Overview of the historical context:** Emancipation, brought about by the Emancipation Proclamation in 1863 and the 13th Amendment in 1865, marked the formal end of slavery in the United States. Reconstruction, the period following the Civil War from 1865 to 1877, aimed to rebuild the South and ensure the rights and freedoms of formerly enslaved individuals.

  - **Challenges of Reconstruction:** Despite the promise of freedom, Reconstruction faced numerous challenges, including widespread violence and resistance from white supremacists, the implementation of discriminatory laws such as Black Codes and Jim Crow laws, and the failure to fully realize the goals of racial equality and justice.

## 2. Literature of Emancipation and

# Reconstruction

- **Overview of literary forms:** Literature produced during and after Emancipation and Reconstruction encompassed a variety of genres, including slave narratives, autobiographies, novels, poetry, and essays. These works provided a platform for formerly enslaved individuals to tell their own stories, assert their humanity, and advocate for their rights.

- **Themes and motifs**: Common themes in literature of this period include the quest for freedom and self-determination, the challenges of rebuilding shattered lives and communities, the persistence of racism and oppression, and the resilience and agency of formerly enslaved individuals in the face of adversity.

# 3. Narratives of Struggle and Triumph

- **Analysis of prominent narratives**: Narrative accounts written by formerly enslaved individuals offer firsthand testimonies of the struggles and triumphs of emancipation and Reconstruction. Works such as "Up from Slavery" by Booker T. Washington, "The Souls of Black Folk" by W.E.B. Du Bois, and "Incidents in the Life of a Slave Girl" by Harriet Jacobs provide vivid and poignant portraits of life before, during, and after slavery.

- **Themes explored**: These narratives explore a range of themes, including the brutality of slavery, the challenges of emancipation and Reconstruction, the quest for education and self-improvement, and the ongoing fight for justice and equality in the face of persistent racism and discrimination.

- **Impact of these narratives:** The publication of these narratives helped to humanize the experiences of formerly enslaved individuals, challenge prevailing stereotypes and misconceptions, and mobilize support for the goals of emancipation and Reconstruction. These narratives played a crucial role in shaping public opinion and influencing political debates about the future of race relations in America.

# 4. Literary Responses to Reconstruction

- **Novels and poetry**: In addition to autobiographical narratives, literature of the Reconstruction era included novels and poetry that addressed the social, political, and economic challenges of the post-Civil War South. Works such as "The Marrow of Tradition" by Charles W. Chesnutt and "The Colored Patriots of the American Revolution" by William Cooper Nell provided fictional and poetic accounts of the struggles and triumphs of African Americans during this turbulent period.

- **Themes explored**: These works explored themes such as interracial relations, political corruption, economic exploitation, and the legacy of slavery and racism in American society. Through their vivid characters and compelling storylines, these novels and poems shed light on the complexities of Reconstruction and its lasting impact on American history.

# 5. Legacy of Emancipation and Reconstruction Literature

- **Enduring relevance**: Literature produced during and after Emancipation and Reconstruction continues to resonate with readers today, offering valuable insights into the ongoing struggles for freedom, justice, and equality in America. The narratives of formerly enslaved individuals serve as reminders of the resilience and agency of those who fought for their freedom and dignity in the face of overwhelming odds.

- **Continued challenges**: Despite the progress made during Reconstruction, the legacies of slavery and racism continue to shape American society in profound ways. Literature of this period reminds us of the unfinished work of Reconstruction and the ongoing struggle for racial justice and equality in America.

# 6. Conclusion

- Recap of key themes and contributions: Literature produced during and after Emancipation and Reconstruction offers invaluable insights into the struggles, triumphs, and complex legacies of this transformative era in American history. The narratives of formerly enslaved individuals provide firsthand testimonies of the challenges and triumphs of emancipation and Reconstruction, while novels and other literary works offer nuanced perspectives on the social, political, and cultural dynamics of the period. Themes of resilience, resistance, and identity emerge prominently in these texts, illustrating the multifaceted experiences of African Americans and other marginalized communities during this time of profound change. Moreover, literature from this era contributes to our understanding of the enduring legacies of slavery, segregation, and racial injustice, as well as the ongoing struggles for civil rights and equality. Through the power of storytelling and artistic expression, these works continue to resonate with contemporary audiences, inspiring reflection, dialogue, and action towards a more just and equitable society.

# Chapter 8: Oral Traditions and Folklore

Oral traditions and folklore have long served as vital means of preserving cultural heritage, transmitting knowledge, and fostering community cohesion across generations. In the context of African American culture, these traditions have played a particularly significant role in shaping identity, resisting oppression, and affirming resilience in the face of adversity. In this chapter, we will explore the rich tapestry of oral traditions and folklore within African American communities, examining the ways in which storytelling, folk tales, legends, and oral histories have been passed down through generations.

## 1. Introduction to Oral Traditions and Folklore

- **Overview of oral traditions:** Oral traditions encompass a wide range of cultural practices, including storytelling, folk songs, proverbs, riddles, and oral histories, passed down orally from one generation to the next. These traditions serve as repositories of cultural knowledge, values, and beliefs, providing insights into the lived experiences of a community and its collective identity.

- **Importance of folklore:** Folklore, the expressive culture of a community, encompasses myths, legends, folk tales, and rituals that reflect the beliefs, values, and social norms of a society. Folklore serves as a mirror of a community's collective imagination, offering insights into its worldview, cosmology, and social organization.

# 2. Storytelling as Cultural Heritage

- **Role of storytelling:** Storytelling is a fundamental aspect of human communication, serving as a means of entertainment, education, and cultural transmission. Within African American communities, storytelling has played a central role in preserving cultural memory, affirming identity, and resisting oppression.

- **Analysis of storytelling traditions:** African American storytelling traditions draw on a rich tapestry of cultural influences, including African, European, and Indigenous traditions. These stories often blend elements of myth, legend, and personal narrative to create vibrant and dynamic narratives that reflect the complexities of African American experiences.

# 3. Folk Tales and Legends

- **Overview of folk tales:** Folk tales are traditional narratives passed down orally from one generation to the next. These tales often feature archetypal characters, motifs, and themes that resonate across cultures and time periods.

- **Analysis of African American folk tales:** African American folk tales draw on a diverse range of cultural influences, including African, European, and Indigenous traditions. These tales often feature trickster figures, such as Br'er Rabbit and Anansi the Spider, who outsmart more powerful adversaries through cunning and wit. Other common themes include the power of community, the importance of resourcefulness, and the triumph of the underdog.

# 4. Oral Histories and Personal Narratives

- **Importance of oral histories:** Oral histories provide firsthand accounts of historical events, personal experiences, and cultural practices passed down through generations. These narratives offer valuable insights into the lived experiences of individuals and communities, as well as the social and cultural contexts in which they unfold.

    - **Analysis of oral histories within African American communities**: African American oral histories encompass a wide range of experiences, from stories of survival and resilience during slavery to accounts of migration, urbanization, and social change in the 20th century. These narratives provide a window into the diverse and dynamic experiences of African Americans across time and place.

# 5. The Role of Folklore in Resistance and Resilience

- **Resistance through folklore**: Folklore has long served as a tool for resistance and resilience within African American communities, providing a means of preserving cultural identity, fostering community solidarity, and challenging dominant narratives of oppression. Stories of trickster figures, for example, often reflect strategies of survival and resistance in the face of adversity.

    - **Resilience through folklore:** Folklore also serves as a source of resilience and empowerment, offering narratives of triumph over adversity and the power of collective action. Through folk tales, legends, and oral histories, African American communities affirm their resilience, agency, and cultural pride in the face of systemic injustice and inequality.

# 6. Conclusion

- Recap of key themes and contributions: Oral traditions and folklore have played a vital role in preserving cultural heritage, transmitting knowledge, and fostering resilience within African American communities. Storytelling, folk tales, legends, and oral histories serve as repositories of cultural memory, offering insights into the lived experiences of individuals and communities across generations.

- Reflection on the enduring relevance of oral traditions: Oral traditions continue to shape African American culture and identity, providing a source of connection, empowerment, and resilience in the face of ongoing challenges. By engaging with the stories, folk tales, and oral histories of the past, African American communities affirm their rich cultural heritage and reaffirm their commitment to justice, equality, and cultural preservation.

# Chapter 9: Gender and Slavery

The intersection of gender and slavery presents a complex and often overlooked aspect of the institution of slavery in America. Enslaved women experienced unique forms of oppression and exploitation, shaped by the intersecting forces of race, gender, and power dynamics. In this chapter, we will examine the distinct experiences of enslaved women and their representation in literature, analyzing works that shed light on the multifaceted nature of their experiences.

## 1. Introduction to Gender and Slavery

- **Overview of the intersectionality of slavery:** Slavery was not a monolithic experience, but rather a complex system of oppression shaped by intersecting factors such as race, gender, class, and nationality. Enslaved women faced unique challenges and vulnerabilities within this system, as their bodies and labor were subjected to exploitation and control by both slaveholders and patriarchal norms.

- **Importance of gender analysis:** Gender analysis provides a lens through which to understand the specific ways in which slavery impacted women's lives, identities, and agency. By examining the experiences of enslaved women, we can gain a deeper understanding of the complexities of power dynamics and resistance within the institution of slavery.

# 2. Representation of Enslaved Women in Literature

- **Overview of literary representations**: Literature has played a crucial role in shaping public perceptions of slavery and its impact on women's lives. Works of fiction, nonfiction, and poetry offer insights into the experiences of enslaved women, from their roles within the household to their struggles for freedom and autonomy.

- **Analysis of key themes**: Literature addressing the experiences of enslaved women often explores themes such as sexual exploitation and violence, motherhood and family, resistance and resilience, and the quest for freedom and dignity. These works provide nuanced and multifaceted portrayals of enslaved women's lives, challenging stereotypes and misconceptions about their experiences.

# 3. The Double Oppression of Enslaved Women

- **Sexual exploitation and violence**: Enslaved women were particularly vulnerable to sexual exploitation and violence at the hands of slaveholders, overseers, and other men in positions of power. Rape, sexual assault, and forced reproduction were common tactics used to exert control over enslaved women's bodies and labor.

- **Motherhood and family**: Despite the harsh realities of slavery, enslaved women often found ways to create and maintain family bonds and support networks. Motherhood held particular significance for enslaved women, as they navigated the challenges of raising children in the midst of oppression and violence.

# 4. Resistance and Resilience of Enslaved Women

- **Acts of resistance**: Enslaved women engaged in a variety of forms of resistance, from acts of sabotage and rebellion to covert acts of defiance and subversion. Through their resilience and resourcefulness, enslaved women asserted their humanity and agency in the face of overwhelming oppression.

   - **Spiritual and cultural resistance:** Religion and spirituality provided important sources of strength and resilience for enslaved women, who drew on African traditions, Christian beliefs, and communal rituals to cope with the traumas of slavery and envision a better future.

# 5. Literary Works on Gender and Slavery

- **Analysis of literary works**: Literature addressing the intersection of gender and slavery offers rich and diverse perspectives on the experiences of enslaved women. Works such as "Incidents in the Life of a Slave Girl" by Harriet Jacobs, "Beloved" by Toni Morrison, and "The Color Purple" by Alice Walker provide nuanced and powerful portrayals of the struggles and triumphs of enslaved women.

   - **Themes explored**: These works explore a range of themes, including the impact of sexual violence on women's lives, the bonds of sisterhood and solidarity, the legacy of trauma and resilience, and the quest for freedom and self-determination.

# 6. Conclusion

- **Recap of key themes and contributions:** The intersection of gender and slavery presents a complex and often overlooked aspect of American history. Enslaved women faced unique forms of oppression and exploitation, shaped by intersecting forces of race, gender, and power dynamics. Literature addressing this intersection provides valuable insights into the experiences of enslaved women, shedding light on their struggles, resilience, and agency within the institution of slavery.

- **Reflection on the enduring relevance of gender and slavery:** The stories of enslaved women continue to resonate with readers today, offering valuable perspectives on the ongoing struggles for gender equity, racial justice, and human rights. By engaging with the literature and experiences of enslaved women, we can gain a deeper understanding of the complexities of power dynamics and resistance within systems of oppression.

# Chapter 10: Resistance in Religion

Religion played a multifaceted role in the lives of enslaved individuals in America, serving as both a source of oppression and a beacon of hope and resistance. Despite the efforts of slaveholders to manipulate and control religious beliefs and practices, enslaved people found ways to reinterpret and reclaim their faith as a means of asserting their humanity and resisting their oppressors. In this chapter, we will explore the role of religion in providing hope and strength to enslaved individuals, and analyze spirituals, sermons, and religious texts as forms of resistance literature.

## 1. The Role of Religion in the Lives of Enslaved Individuals

- **Overview of religion in slavery**: Religion was a central aspect of life for many enslaved individuals in America, providing a framework for understanding the world, coping with adversity, and finding meaning and purpose in the midst of suffering. Enslaved people drew on a variety of religious traditions, including Christianity, Islam, and African spiritual practices, to navigate the challenges of slavery and assert their humanity.

- **Manipulation and control:** Slaveholders often sought to manipulate and control the religious beliefs and practices of enslaved individuals, using Christianity as a tool of social control and justification for slavery. Enslaved people were often subjected to harsh interpretations of biblical passages that emphasized obedience and submission to authority.

# 2. Spirituals: Songs of Hope and Resistance

- **Overview of spirituals**: Spirituals were religious songs created and sung by enslaved African Americans, often in the context of worship gatherings, prayer meetings, and labor. These songs served as expressions of faith, resilience, and resistance, offering enslaved individuals a means of affirming their humanity and envisioning a future free from oppression.

- **Analysis of key themes:** Spirituals encompass a wide range of themes, including liberation, deliverance, justice, and salvation. Many spirituals contain coded messages and imagery that convey messages of resistance and hope, while others reflect the pain and suffering of enslaved life.

# 3. Sermons: Voices of Resistance and Redemption

- **Overview of sermons**: Sermons delivered by enslaved preachers and religious leaders provided opportunities for enslaved individuals to gather, worship, and find solace in their faith. These sermons often addressed themes of liberation, justice, and the transformative power of God's love, offering hope and strength in the midst of adversity.

- **Analysis of key messages**: Enslaved preachers drew on biblical stories and teachings to inspire and uplift their congregations, emphasizing themes of justice, equality, and divine intervention in the face of oppression. Sermons often served as acts of resistance against the dehumanizing ideologies of slavery, challenging slaveholders' authority and asserting the dignity and worth of enslaved individuals.

# 4. Religious Texts: Sources of Inspiration and Liberation

- Overview of religious texts: Enslaved individuals often found inspiration and solace in religious texts such as the Bible, the Quran, and other sacred texts. These texts provided narratives of liberation, deliverance, and divine justice that resonated deeply with enslaved people's experiences of oppression and longing for freedom.
   - Analysis of key passages: Enslaved individuals interpreted religious texts through the lens of their own experiences, finding parallels between biblical stories of liberation and their own struggles for freedom. Passages such as the Exodus story, the Psalms of lament and deliverance, and the teachings of Jesus on justice and compassion offered hope and encouragement to enslaved individuals in their darkest hours.

# 5. Conclusion

- **Recap of key themes and contributions**: Religion played a complex and often contradictory role in the lives of enslaved individuals in America, serving as both a source of oppression and a means of resistance and liberation. Spirituals, sermons, and religious texts provided enslaved individuals with opportunities to express their faith, assert their humanity, and envision a future free from bondage.

- **Reflection on the enduring legacy of resistance in religion**: The songs, sermons, and texts of enslaved individuals continue to resonate with readers today, offering valuable insights into the power of faith and resilience in the face of oppression. By engaging with the religious traditions of enslaved people, we can gain a deeper understanding of the enduring legacy of resistance and liberation in American history.

# Chapter 11: The Legacy of Resistance

The literature produced during the 19th century, particularly in the context of slavery and the fight for emancipation, continues to resonate deeply in contemporary movements for social justice. The enduring legacy of resistance literature serves as a testament to the power of storytelling, advocacy, and collective action in confronting systemic oppression and inequality. In this chapter, we will examine the lasting impact of 19th-century literature on contemporary movements for social justice and discuss the relevance of these works in understanding and addressing ongoing issues of racism and inequality.

## 1. Introduction to the Legacy of Resistance Literature

- **Overview of 19th-century literature**: The 19th century was a period of profound social, political, and cultural upheaval in America, marked by the struggle for emancipation, the abolitionist movement, and the fight for civil rights. Literature produced during this time played a crucial role in shaping public opinion, inspiring activism, and laying the groundwork for future movements for social justice.

- **Importance of resistance literature**: Resistance literature encompasses a wide range of genres, including slave narratives, abolitionist pamphlets, novels, poetry, and speeches, that challenged the status quo and advocated for radical change. These works provided a platform for marginalized voices to be heard, shedding light on the injustices of slavery, racism, and inequality, and inspiring readers to take action.

# 2. The Impact of 19th-Century Literature on Social Justice Movements

- **Abolitionist literature**: Abolitionist literature, including slave narratives such as Frederick Douglass's "Narrative of the Life of Frederick Douglass" and Harriet Beecher Stowe's "Uncle Tom's Cabin," played a central role in galvanizing support for the abolitionist cause. These works exposed the brutality of slavery, challenged racial stereotypes, and mobilized public opinion against the institution of slavery.

- **Civil rights literature**: The literature of the Reconstruction era, including works by African American authors such as W.E.B. Du Bois and Ida B. Wells, laid the groundwork for the civil rights movement of the 20th century. These works documented the struggles of formerly enslaved individuals and their descendants, advocated for political and social equality, and called attention to the ongoing injustices of segregation and discrimination.

- **Contemporary relevance**: The themes and messages of 19th-century literature remain relevant in contemporary movements for social justice, including the Black Lives Matter movement, the fight for immigrant rights, and the struggle for LGBTQ+ rights. These movements draw inspiration from the courage, resilience, and activism of past generations, while also challenging the persistent legacies of racism, inequality, and injustice in American society.

# 3. Understanding Ongoing Issues of Racism and Inequality

**- Systemic racism**: The literature of the 19th century provides valuable insights into the origins and perpetuation of systemic racism in America. Works such as Douglass's narrative and Stowe's novel expose the ways in which slavery and its legacies continue to shape racial inequality, economic exploitation, and social marginalization in contemporary society.

- **Intersectionality**: 19th-century literature also sheds light on the intersectional nature of oppression, highlighting the ways in which race, gender, class, and other forms of identity intersect to produce systems of privilege and disadvantage. Understanding these intersecting systems of oppression is essential for addressing the complex and interconnected issues of racism and inequality in the 21st century.

- **Collective action**: Perhaps most importantly, the literature of the 19th century serves as a reminder of the power of collective action in confronting injustice and effecting social change. The abolitionist movement, the civil rights movement, and other struggles for liberation were driven by the efforts of individuals and communities working together to challenge the status quo and build a more just and equitable society.

# 4. Conclusion

- **Recap of key themes and contributions:** The literature of the 19th century continues to inspire, inform, and guide contemporary movements for social justice. The themes of resistance, resilience, and collective action embodied in these works serve as a powerful reminder of the ongoing struggle for racial equality, human rights, and dignity in America and around the world.

- **Reflection on the enduring legacy of resistance literature:** By engaging with the literature of the past, we can gain a deeper understanding of the complexities of racism, inequality, and injustice in our society and draw inspiration from the courage and resilience of those who came before us. The legacy of resistance literature reminds us that the fight for justice is ongoing and that we all have a role to play in building a more inclusive and equitable future.

# Chapter 12: Literary Criticism and Interpretation

The study of 19th-century literature of resistance and resilience has undergone significant evolution over time, reflecting changing cultural, social, and intellectual contexts. From its emergence in the immediate aftermath of slavery to contemporary scholarly perspectives, literary criticism and interpretation have played a crucial role in shaping our understanding of the complexities of resistance literature. In this chapter, we will analyze scholarly perspectives on 19th-century literature of resistance and resilience, and discuss the evolution of critical interpretations over time.

## 1. Introduction to Literary Criticism and Interpretation

- **Overview of literary criticism**: Literary criticism is the analysis, interpretation, and evaluation of literary texts, with the aim of understanding their meaning, themes, and stylistic features. Critics draw on a variety of theoretical approaches, methodologies, and interdisciplinary perspectives to interpret literature within its historical, cultural, and social contexts.

    - **Importance of interpretation**: Interpretation is a central aspect of literary criticism, as it involves making sense of a text's meaning and significance through close reading, analysis, and contextualization. Interpretive approaches vary widely depending on the critic's theoretical orientation, methodological framework, and scholarly interests.

# 2. Scholarly Perspectives on 19th-Century Literature of Resistance and Resilience

- **Emergence of literary criticism**: The study of 19th-century literature of resistance and resilience emerged in the late 19th and early 20th centuries, as scholars began to explore the literary and cultural significance of works by authors such as Harriet Beecher Stowe, Frederick Douglass, and Harriet Jacobs. Early critics focused on documenting the historical and social contexts of these works, as well as their impact on contemporary debates about race, slavery, and social justice.

- **Marxist and materialist perspectives**: Marxist and materialist critics in the mid-20th century emphasized the economic and social dimensions of literature, analyzing how literary texts reflect and critique the structures of power and inequality in society. These critics examined 19th-century literature of resistance within the broader context of capitalist exploitation, class struggle, and revolutionary potential.

- **Feminist and gender studies approaches**: Feminist and gender studies scholars in the late 20th and early 21st centuries focused on the experiences and perspectives of marginalized groups, including women, people of color, and LGBTQ+ individuals. These critics explored the ways in which 19th-century literature of resistance addresses issues of gender, race, sexuality, and power, highlighting the intersections of oppression and resistance.

- **Postcolonial and critical race theory perspectives**: Postcolonial and critical race theory scholars in the late 20th and early 21st centuries examined the legacy of colonialism, imperialism, and racism in literature, focusing on the ways in which texts by authors of color challenge dominant narratives and reclaim agency and identity. These critics analyzed 19th-century literature of resistance as part of a broader tradition of decolonization, liberation, and anti-racist activism.

# 3. Evolution of Critical Interpretations Over Time

- **Changing methodologies**: The study of 19th-century literature of resistance has evolved over time, reflecting changes in literary theory, methodological approaches, and scholarly interests. Early critics focused primarily on historical and biographical approaches, seeking to document the social and political contexts of literary works and their impact on contemporary audiences.

  - **Shift towards interdisciplinary perspectives**: In the late 20th and early 21st centuries, literary criticism became increasingly interdisciplinary, drawing on insights from fields such as history, sociology, anthropology, psychology, and cultural studies. Critics began to explore the intersections of literature with other forms of cultural production, including music, art, film, and digital media.

  - **Emphasis on diversity and inclusion**: Contemporary literary criticism places a greater emphasis on diversity, inclusion, and representation, seeking to amplify the voices and experiences of marginalized groups that have been historically excluded or marginalized in literary studies. Critics are increasingly attentive to issues of race, gender, sexuality, class, disability, and nationality, and their intersections in literature of resistance and resilience.

# 4. Conclusion

- **Recap of key themes and contributions**: Literary criticism and interpretation have played a crucial role in shaping our understanding of 19th-century literature of resistance and resilience. From its emergence in the late 19th century to contemporary perspectives informed by interdisciplinary approaches and social justice frameworks, criticism has evolved to reflect changing cultural, social, and intellectual contexts.

- **Reflection on the future of literary criticism:** As literary studies continue to evolve, critics will grapple with new challenges and questions about the nature and significance of literature in an increasingly globalized and interconnected world. By engaging with diverse perspectives, methodologies, and theoretical frameworks, literary criticism can continue to enrich our understanding of literature and its role in shaping our understanding of the world.

# Chapter 13: Adaptations and Reimaginings

The 19th-century slave narratives and literature represent a profound and enduring legacy of resistance and resilience. In contemporary times, these works continue to captivate audiences and inspire creators to adapt and reimagine them for new contexts and audiences. From film adaptations to graphic novels, from stage plays to digital media, modern adaptations of 19th-century slave narratives and literature offer a rich and complex tapestry of reinterpretations that reflect changing attitudes and perspectives towards issues of race, identity, and social justice. In this chapter, we will explore the landscape of modern adaptations of 19th-century slave narratives and literature, and analyze how these reinterpretations reflect evolving cultural, social, and political contexts.

## 1. Introduction to Adaptations and Reimaginings

- **Overview of adaptation**: Adaptation is the process of transforming a literary text into a new form, such as film, theater, visual art, or digital media. Adaptations allow creators to reinterpret and reimagine classic works for contemporary audiences, offering new insights and perspectives on familiar stories.

 - **Importance of adaptation:** Adaptations of 19th-century slave narratives and literature provide opportunities to engage with these works in fresh and innovative ways, reaching new audiences and sparking conversations about their relevance to contemporary issues of race, identity, and social justice.

## 2. Modern Film Adaptations

- **Overview of film adaptations:** Film adaptations of 19th-century slave narratives and literature have been particularly influential in shaping public perceptions of slavery and its legacies. From classic Hollywood productions to independent films, filmmakers have sought to bring these stories to life on the big screen, often with mixed results.

- **Analysis of key adaptations:** Notable film adaptations include "12 Years a Slave" (2013), directed by Steve McQueen and based on Solomon Northup's memoir, and "Beloved" (1998), directed by Jonathan Demme and based on Toni Morrison's novel. These films offer powerful and visceral portrayals of the brutality of slavery, while also exploring themes of resilience, resistance, and redemption.

## 3. Stage Plays and Theater Adaptations

- **Overview of theater adaptations**: Stage plays and theater adaptations of 19th-century slave narratives and literature provide opportunities for live performance and audience engagement, offering a visceral and immersive experience that brings these stories to life in a new way.

- **Analysis of key adaptations**: Notable theater adaptations include "The Color Purple" (2005), a musical based on Alice Walker's novel, and "The Underground Railroad Game" (2016), a provocative and experimental play that explores the legacy of slavery and its impact on contemporary society. These adaptations challenge audiences to confront uncomfortable truths about the past while also celebrating the resilience and agency of enslaved individuals.

# 4. Graphic Novels and Visual Adaptations

- **Overview of graphic novels**: Graphic novels and visual adaptations of 19th-century slave narratives and literature offer a unique combination of text and imagery, providing a visual interpretation of these stories that can be particularly powerful and evocative.

   - **Analysis of key adaptations**: Notable graphic novels include "March" (2013-2016), written by John Lewis and Andrew Aydin and illustrated by Nate Powell, which tells the story of the Civil Rights Movement through the eyes of Congressman John Lewis. Another example is "Kindred: A Graphic Novel Adaptation" (2017), adapted by Damian Duffy and illustrated by John Jennings, which reimagines Octavia Butler's classic novel as a visually stunning and emotionally resonant graphic narrative.

# 5. Digital Media and New Technologies

- **Overview of digital media**: Digital media and new technologies offer innovative ways to adapt and reinterpret 19th-century slave narratives and literature, allowing creators to reach new audiences and engage with these stories in interactive and immersive ways.

   - **Analysis of key adaptations**: Notable examples include virtual reality experiences such as "The Middle Passage VR" (2018), which immerses users in the harrowing journey of enslaved Africans across the Atlantic Ocean, and interactive websites such as "The Douglass Project" (2020), which explores the life and legacy of Frederick Douglass through multimedia storytelling and archival materials.

# 6. Conclusion

- **Recap of key themes and contributions**: Modern adaptations of 19th-century slave narratives and literature offer a rich and diverse array of reinterpretations that reflect changing attitudes and perspectives towards issues of race, identity, and social justice. From film adaptations to graphic novels, from stage plays to digital media, these adaptations engage with familiar stories in innovative and thought-provoking ways, inviting audiences to reconsider their understanding of the past and its relevance to the present.

- **Reflection on the enduring legacy of adaptation:** By adapting and reimagining 19th-century slave narratives and literature, creators continue to breathe new life into these timeless stories, ensuring that they remain relevant and resonant for future generations. These adaptations serve as a testament to the enduring power of storytelling and the ongoing struggle for justice, freedom, and equality in America and around the world.

# Chapter 14: Educational Significance

In recent years, there has been a growing recognition of the importance of incorporating literature of resistance into educational curricula. These texts offer profound insights into historical injustices, social struggles, and the resilience of marginalized communities. By studying literature of resistance, students gain a deeper understanding of the complexities of power dynamics, systemic oppression, and the ongoing fight for justice. This chapter will explore the educational significance of integrating such literature into curricula, analyzing teaching strategies and resources to effectively engage students with these texts.

## The Importance of Literature of Resistance in Education

Literature of resistance encompasses a diverse range of works, including novels, poetry, memoirs, and essays, produced by individuals and communities who have confronted oppression and advocated for change. These texts serve as powerful tools for challenging dominant narratives, fostering empathy, and empowering students to critically examine the world around them.

One of the primary reasons for incorporating literature of resistance into educational curricula is its ability to amplify marginalized voices. Traditional curricula often prioritize canonical texts that reflect the perspectives of dominant groups, neglecting the experiences and struggles of marginalized communities. By introducing students to literature of resistance, educators provide them with access to alternative narratives and perspectives, enriching their understanding of history and society.

Furthermore, literature of resistance encourages students to grapple with complex social issues, such as racism, sexism, colonialism, and economic inequality. Through the analysis of these texts, students develop critical thinking skills and learn to interrogate power structures, fostering a sense of social responsibility and civic engagement.

Moreover, literature of resistance has the power to inspire and empower students. By encountering stories of resilience, resistance, and triumph in the face of adversity, students gain a sense of agency and hope. These texts not only validate the experiences of marginalized individuals but also instill a belief in the possibility of creating positive change.

## Teaching Strategies for Engaging Students

Effectively teaching literature of resistance requires careful planning and consideration of students' diverse backgrounds and experiences. The following are some strategies for engaging students with these texts:

**1. Cultivating a Culturally Responsive Classroom:** Create a classroom environment that honors and respects students' diverse identities and experiences. Incorporate texts that reflect a variety of cultural perspectives and invite students to share their own stories and insights.

**2. Fostering Critical Dialogue:** Encourage open and respectful discussions about the themes, characters, and historical contexts of literature of resistance. Provide opportunities for students to critically analyze the texts and challenge their own assumptions and biases.

**3. Utilizing Multimodal Resources:** Supplement written texts with multimedia resources, such as videos, music, artwork, and primary sources. This allows students to engage with the material in different ways and enhances their understanding of complex historical and social issues.

**4. Promoting Empathy and Perspective-Taking:** Help students develop empathy by inviting them to imagine themselves in the shoes of the characters and communities depicted in literature of resistance. Encourage them to consider how historical events and social structures have shaped individuals' lives and experiences.

**5. Encouraging Creative Expression:** Provide opportunities for students to express themselves creatively through writing, art, performance, or other mediums. Encourage them to create their own works inspired by the themes and messages of literature of resistance, fostering a sense of agency and self-expression.

# Resources for Teaching Literature of Resistance

There is a wealth of resources available to educators for teaching literature of resistance. Some key resources include:

**1. Anthologies**: Anthologies compile a diverse range of literary works by authors from marginalized communities. Examples include "The Norton Anthology of African American Literature" and "Latinx Literature: A Critical Anthology."

**2. Educator Guides:** Many publishers and educational organizations provide educator guides and teaching materials specifically designed for incorporating literature of resistance into the curriculum. These guides often include discussion questions, lesson plans, and supplementary resources.

**3. Digital Archives**: Digital archives, such as the Digital Public Library of America and the Library of Congress's Chronicling America, provide access to a wide range of primary sources, including newspapers, photographs, letters, and other documents related to social movements and resistance.

**4. Online Discussion Platforms:** Online platforms, such as forums, blogs, and social media groups, provide opportunities for educators to connect with colleagues and share teaching strategies, lesson plans, and recommended readings related to literature of resistance.

**5. Community Partnerships:** Partner with local community organizations, cultural institutions, and activists to bring literature of resistance into the classroom. Guest speakers, field trips, and collaborative projects can enrich students' learning experiences and connect them with real-world social justice efforts.

## Conclusion

Incorporating literature of resistance into educational curricula is essential for fostering critical thinking, empathy, and social responsibility among students. By studying these texts, students gain a deeper understanding of historical injustices, systemic oppression, and the ongoing struggles for justice and equality. Through thoughtful teaching strategies and the use of diverse resources, educators can effectively engage students with literature of resistance, empowering them to become agents of positive change in their communities and beyond.

## Chapter 15: Conclusion

# Recap of Key Themes and Findings

Throughout this exploration of literature of resistance and resilience in 19th-century America, several key themes and findings have emerged. These themes not only highlight the struggles and triumphs of marginalized communities during this period but also underscore the enduring relevance of literature of resistance in shaping social consciousness and fostering resilience.

**1. Historical Context**: The 19th century was a time of profound social, political, and economic change in America. The nation grappled with issues such as slavery, westward expansion, industrialization, and immigration, which shaped the experiences of individuals and communities across the country.

**2. Systemic Oppression:** Literature of resistance exposes the systemic oppression and injustices faced by marginalized communities, including African Americans, Indigenous peoples, women, immigrants, and laborers. These texts shed light on the dehumanizing effects of slavery, colonization, racism, sexism, and economic exploitation, challenging dominant narratives and calling for social change.

**3. Resilience and Resistance:** Despite facing immense obstacles, marginalized communities demonstrated remarkable resilience and resistance. Through acts of defiance, solidarity, and creative expression, individuals and communities asserted their humanity, reclaimed their dignity, and fought for justice and equality.

**4. Cultural Production**: Literature of resistance encompasses a diverse range of cultural production, including slave narratives, abolitionist literature, Indigenous oral traditions, feminist writings, immigrant narratives, and labor songs. These texts reflect the diverse experiences, voices, and perspectives of marginalized communities, enriching our understanding of American history and culture.

**5. Legacy and Impact:** The literature of resistance produced during the 19th century continues to have a profound impact on contemporary society. These texts have inspired social movements, influenced public discourse, and shaped cultural attitudes towards issues of race, gender, class, and identity. Moreover, they serve as a testament to the resilience, creativity, and humanity of those who have struggled against oppression and injustice.

# Reflection on the Enduring Relevance of Literature of Resistance and Resilience

The literature of resistance and resilience produced in 19th-century America remains as relevant and vital today as it was during its time. In an era marked by ongoing struggles for justice, equality, and human rights, these texts offer valuable insights and inspiration for confronting contemporary challenges and envisioning a more just and equitable society.

**1. Challenging Dominant Narratives**: Literature of resistance challenges dominant narratives and exposes the complexities of American history and society. By centering the voices and experiences of marginalized communities, these texts disrupt the myth of American exceptionalism and highlight the ongoing legacy of oppression and resistance.

**2. Inspiring Social Justice Movements**: The literature of resistance serves as a source of inspiration and empowerment for contemporary social justice movements. From the civil rights movement to the #MeToo movement, activists and organizers have drawn upon the writings and legacies of past struggles to mobilize communities, build solidarity, and demand change.

**3. Fostering Empathy and Understanding:** By engaging with literature of resistance, readers gain a deeper understanding of the experiences and struggles of marginalized communities. These texts invite readers to empathize with the pain, resilience, and humanity of those who have been marginalized and oppressed, fostering a sense of solidarity and compassion across difference.

**4. Promoting Cultural Preservation and Revitalization**: For Indigenous communities, literature of resistance plays a crucial role in preserving and revitalizing cultural traditions, languages, and knowledge systems. Indigenous oral traditions, storytelling, and literature serve as a means of transmitting ancestral wisdom, resisting colonial erasure, and reclaiming cultural identity and sovereignty.

**5. Empowering Marginalized Voices:** Literature of resistance empowers marginalized voices and validates the lived experiences of those who have been historically silenced and marginalized. By amplifying these voices, these texts challenge systems of power and privilege, affirming the dignity and worth of all individuals and communities.

In conclusion, the literature of resistance and resilience produced in 19th-century America continues to resonate with contemporary audiences, offering valuable lessons and insights for navigating the complexities of the present moment. By engaging with these texts, we honor the struggles and triumphs of those who have come before us and reaffirm our commitment to building a more just, equitable, and inclusive society for future generations. As we reflect on the enduring relevance of literature of resistance, let us be inspired to continue the ongoing work of social justice and liberation, drawing strength from the resilience and resistance of those who have paved the way before us.

# Don't miss out!

Visit the website below and you can sign up to receive emails whenever Nora Hayes publishes a new book. There's no charge and no obligation.

https://books2read.com/r/B-A-QWKJB-EBLED

**BOOKS 2 READ**

Connecting independent readers to independent writers.

# About the Author

Nora Hayes, an accomplished American author, crafts narratives that delve into the human experience and the essence of Americana. With a background rooted in the heartland, Hayes explores themes of identity, belonging, and the ever-shifting landscape of life. Her work is characterized by evocative prose and compelling characters, resonating with readers on a profound level. As a seasoned voice in contemporary American literature, Hayes continues to shape the literary landscape, offering insight into the complexities of existence and the enduring power of storytelling.